7-18

STATE BIRDS

STATE BIRDS

illustrations by Arthur Singer and Alan Singer

text by Virginia Buckley

LODESTAR BOOKS   DUTTON   NEW YORK

to my wife, Dale, and to my sons, Paul and Alan

ARTHUR SINGER

with deepest respect for my parents, Arthur
and Edith, and the artistic gifts they have nurtured,
and special thanks to my wife, Anna, and son,
Nathaniel

ALAN SINGER

Where an individual bird is portrayed, it is always the male. The
two yellowhammers pictured on page 9 are males.

Females are shown on the following pages: 11, bottom; 16–17,
first and fourth birds; 18, right; 29, bottom; 30; 32–33, first and
fourth birds; 40, top; 45, top; 46, right; 58–59, first and second
birds.

In all other paintings showing more than one bird, the male and
female are practically indistinguishable in the field.

Text copyright © 1986 by Virginia Buckley
Illustrations copyright © 1986 by Arthur Singer and Alan Singer
All rights reserved.
Unicorn is a registered trademark of Dutton
Library of Congress number 86-2209
ISBN: 0-525-67314-8
Published in the United States by Lodestar Books,
an affiliate of Dutton Children's Books,
a division of Penguin Books USA Inc.
Published simultaneously in Canada by
Fitzhenry & Whiteside Limited, Toronto
Designer: Riki Levinson
Printed in Hong Kong by South China Printing Co.
First Lodestar Unicorn Edition 1990
10 9 8 7 6 5 4 3 2 1

frontispiece:
bald eagle, *Haliaeetus leucocephalus*
United States emblem

THE NATIONAL AUDUBON SOCIETY AND ITS MISSION

The National Audubon Society, with more than half a million members, 500 chapters, 10 regional offices, a $25 million budget, and a staff of 273, is a powerful force for conservation research, education, and action.

The Society's headquarters are in New York City; the legislative branch works out of an office on Capitol Hill in Washington, D.C. Ecology camps, environmental education centers, research stations, and 80 sanctuaries are strategically located throughout the country. The Society publishes *Audubon* magazine, *American Birds, Audubon Action,* and *Audubon Adventures,* a newsletter that is part of the youth education program.

The Society's mission is expressed by the Audubon Cause: to conserve plants and animals and their habitats, to further the wise use of land and water, to promote rational energy strategies, to protect life from pollution, and to seek solutions to global environmental problems.

National Audubon Society
950 Third Avenue   New York, New York 10022

Trademark National Audubon Society is used by publisher under license from the National Audubon Society, Inc.

NATIONAL WILDLIFE FEDERATION

The National Wildlife Federation is "Working for the Nature of Tomorrow" and is a leading voice for the conservation of natural resources in America. The Federation urges you to enjoy nature, discover its wonders, and support responsible actions on its behalf.

National Wildlife Federation
1412 Sixteenth Street NW   Washington, D.C. 20036

Contents

Yellowhammer   *Colaptes auratus*

The yellow-shafted flicker, as Alabama's state bird is widely known, lives among trees. Like other woodpeckers, it indicates its presence by loudly tapping on limbs, tree trunks, or even tin roofs. This bird often feeds on the ground, hammering into burrows for ants, its favorite food, and extending its long, sticky tongue to lap up the meal. In their resolution of 1927, Alabama legislators followed tradition in designating this bird by its colloquial name, yellowhammer—one of many affectionate nicknames.

Willow Ptarmigan   *Lagopus lagopus*

The willow ptarmigan, chosen by schoolchildren in a contest held by the Territorial Department of Education in 1955, continues to be the emblem of the state of Alaska. It is a chickenlike land bird, widely distributed throughout the barren lands and willow scrub of the Arctic.

Ptarmigans have two completely different plumages, offering them a unique protective camouflage all year long. In winter, the feathers are pure white, blending in with the snow-covered land. As spring approaches and the snow begins to melt, the feathers undergo several changes to an earthen brown. Often the females molt earlier than the males, giving them extra protection from predators during the nesting season.

Cactus Wren *Campylorhynchus brunneicapillus*

A bird of the desert, the vocal cactus wren, was chosen Arizona's emblem in 1931 at the urging of the State Federation of Women's Clubs. It frequently makes its home in the branches of the spiny cholla or giant saguaro, where it sings all day long in a low-pitched tone. The male will sometimes build several nests. Then the female selects the best-made—and most hidden—nest for the brood. Wrens are solitary and like to roost in nooks and crannies at night when not in their dome-shaped nests.

A close relative, the winter wren, is popular in folktales and appears as king of the birds in medieval celebrations and legends, some of which still persist.

Mockingbird   *Mimus polyglottos*

Famed for its mimicry of the songs of other birds, the mockingbird was designated by Florida in 1927. The same year, proud Texans resolved:

> Whereas, ornithologists, musicians, educators, and Texans in all walks of life unite in proclaiming the mockingbird the most appropriate species for the state bird of Texas, as it is found in all parts of the state, in winter and in summer, in the city and in the country, on the prairie and in the woods and hills, and is a singer of distinctive type, a fighter for the protection of his home, falling, if need be, in its defense, like any true Texan...

Women's clubs voted it in Arkansas in 1929. Its growing popularity led the Tennessee Ornithological Society to mount a campaign in 1933 for its election in that state and Mississippi to adopt it in 1944. The mockingbird is quick to pick up any song it hears, and imitates many other sounds. It sings all year long, usually from a high, exposed perch.

California Quail *Lophortyx californicus*

The California quail, a prized game bird long associated with the state but not officially designated an emblem until 1943, has come a long way since the days when it was hunted and sold by the millions in the markets of San Francisco and Los Angeles. Originally an inhabitant of the lowlands and valleys, it was forced to move when these areas

were cleared for grazing. Conservationists introduced it to city parks, where semi-tame coveys now freely roam. They are a striking sight, especially the male with his jaunty plume and black face bordered by a white band. Quail are monogamous and, fortunately, quite prolific. Two or three broods may be raised a season. The families remain in flocks—which number in the hundreds—throughout the year.

Lark Bunting   *Calamospiza melanocorys*

Controversy and confusion accompanied Colorado's choice of a bird emblem. In 1928, schoolchildren in just one county voted for the lark bunting. The following year, the superintendent of schools arranged for children in all the schools to vote, and the meadowlark was the popular choice. But the lark bunting had somehow been left off the ballot, so a new contest was held, this time with a third entrant, the bluebird, joining the fray. The debate continued until 1931, when legislation was passed naming the lark bunting the state bird.

During the mating season, the prairie grasslands come alive as the gregarious little males—whose crisp black-and-white markings made them such a favorite—flutter and trill their songs for their drab brown mates.

American Robin *Turdus migratorius*

No bird is as familiar and dearly loved as the American robin. Once a forest dweller, it now prefers to nest in cities and suburbs throughout North America, where it is annually welcomed as the traditional herald of spring. The spotted breast of the young, which hatch from clear blue eggs, is evidence of the bird's close relationship to thrushes. Colonists first called this bird the robin in remembrance of their own similar and beloved English bird.

In a contest conducted by the Michigan Audubon Society in 1931, "Robin Red Breast received many more votes than any other bird as the most popular bird in Michigan." Connecticut adopted it in 1943. Wisconsin designated it in 1949, many years after a vote by schoolchildren there. Most robins migrate to the south when the ground freezes because they can no longer feed on earthworms, one of the staples of their diet.

Blue Hen Chicken *Gallus gallus var.*

According to Delaware tradition, during the Revolutionary War, a company of soldiers from Kent County took with them fighting game-cocks said to be the brood of a famous blue hen that had been brought over to the colonies by the first settlers. Matches between these birds provided amusement, and soon the valorous soldiers themselves were nicknamed Blue Hen's Chickens. A Wilmington newspaper bore the name, and it was again carried by a Kent County militia in the Civil War. The nickname has endured on both the state and governor's flags, and in political campaigns throughout the years. When the blue hen chicken was officially adopted as Delaware's bird in 1939, the name was conveniently streamlined.

The raising of gamecocks for fighting goes back to primitive times and is probably more responsible for the spread and domestication of these birds than is their use for meat or eggs. Today's fighting cocks bear a strong resemblance to the ancestral stock, but the true origin of the proverbial blue hen remains a mystery. Indeed, the original bird no longer exists.

Brown Thrasher   *Toxostoma rufum*

The brown thrasher belongs to the family of birds known as Mimidae—mimics—and is a close relative of the mockingbird. However, it mimics the songs of fewer birds than the mockingbird and is limited in the length of its phrases. It sings from protected cover, usually in or near thickets, where it lives close to the ground, eating insects, fruits, and berries. Its breast is streaked with brown, and because of this, it is sometimes confused with the wood thrush. The inquisitive thrashers, who look and act like overgrown wrens, probably developed from a similar thrushlike ancestor.

Georgia's 1935 resolution naming the brown thrasher its state bird was not made into law until thirty-five years later, in 1970. Thus Georgia was the next-to-last state to adopt a bird, beating New York by two months.

Hawaiian Goose (Nene)   *Branta sandvicensis*

In 1957, two years before statehood, when the Territory of Hawaii adopted the Hawaiian goose, also called the nene (pronounced nay-nay), the bird was close to extinction. A rare species, nenes probably numbered in the thousands before overhunting and wild animals all but destroyed them. Thanks to a restoration project begun in 1949, today the population has increased to many hundreds. Some live in the desolate lava country between Mauna Kea and Mauna Loa, under the partial protection of a national park. Others are being bred in captivity on the United States mainland and in Europe. These ancient birds, who live on the lava flows, are a good example of how creatures can adapt to their environment. Over time, their webbed feet have been transformed to a clawlike shape and their wing structure has been modified for shorter flights.

Mountain Bluebird   *Sialia currucoides*

At home in western mountainous regions, the aptly named mountain bluebird is the emblem of two neighboring states—Idaho, which chose it in 1931, and Nevada, where legislation designating it was enacted in 1967. Reaching into northwestern Canada during the nesting season, this bird is typically found at high elevations, wandering up to twelve thousand feet by the end of summer before returning to lower elevations for winter. The mountain bluebird lacks the rusty breast of the western and eastern species.

Bluebirds belong to the large family of thrushes, as do robins, nightingales, and wheatears—all renowned for their fine singing. Gentler in manner and a softer songster than other thrushes, the bluebird has endeared itself as the bird of happiness in countless songs and stories.

Cardinal   *Cardinalis cardinalis*

The showy cardinal, admired for its "bright plumage and cheerful song," has the double distinction of being both the most popular emblem and also the very first bird to be given official recognition. Kentucky conferred this honor in 1926. The brilliant redbird has adapted to suburban lands, where shrubbery is dominant. It can be found at feeding stations even in winter. Three midwestern states have designated the cardinal—Illinois in 1929, and Indiana and Ohio in 1933. North Carolinians chose it in 1943, after canvassing bird clubs, garden clubs, and many schools. Civic organizations and pupils in public schools sponsored it in West Virginia, leading to a resolution by the 1949 legislature. And Virginia's 1950 resolution, quoted above, leaves no doubt as to why this favorite was "worthy of selection."

American Goldfinch   *Carduelis tristis*

Pastures filled with wildflowers beckon to flocks of goldfinches, which sweep from bloom to bloom, feasting on seeds and flowers. Dandelions, sunflowers, and especially thistles are favored, hence the scientific name of these dainty birds, *Carduelis,* from the Latin *carduus,* a thistle. The birds use thistledown to line their nests. But the plants do not provide nesting material until late summer, so mating is delayed. In autumn, the male doffs his breeding plumage and takes on a grayish yellow color like that of his mate and chicks. Iowa adopted this bird, also known as the eastern goldfinch and, familiarly, the wild canary, in 1933. New Jersey designated it in 1935, and Washington in 1951.

Western Meadowlark *Sturnella neglecta*

At home in open fields and prairies, the western meadowlark "is a bird of beautiful plumage and sweet voice, not destructive by nature, and a typical western bird, native to every section of our state." So proclaimed Oregon's governor in 1927. Earlier in the year, an essay written by a boy in a Wyoming rural school gave impetus to the movement endorsing the bird in that state. A resolution of the Nebraska Federation of Women's Clubs led to a vote by schoolchildren in Nebraska in 1929. And two years later, Montana schoolchildren also chose it. The resolutions of Kansas in 1937 and North Dakota in 1947 brought the total to six states, making the meadowlark the second most popular emblem.

The western and eastern meadowlark are almost identical, but they rarely hybridize—mate with each other. When both species nest in the same field, it is only by the western meadowlark's "sweet voice" that the female can distinguish her mate. The western meadowlark's appetite for locusts and other harmful insects has given it the reputation of being helpful to farmers.

Brown Pelican   *Pelecanus occidentalis*

For many years appearing on the seal of the state of Louisiana, the brown pelican was given official recognition in 1966, the only marine bird to carry this honor. A remarkable if ungainly bird, the pelican is well adapted to life on the coastal marshes. Making vertical, headfirst dives into the water, it scoops up with its enormous pouch the several pounds of fish it requires daily. The pouch also serves as a dip net to drain out the water. Pelicans fly in long lines, sometimes in formation, and are fond of military precision even while resting.

Pelican bones found in deposits 30 to 40 million years old are similar to those of living species. The Greeks and Romans called these birds pelicans or *pelecans*. To the Spanish and Portuguese, they are *alcatraz,* which is also the name of a rocky island in San Francisco Bay that once housed a flock—and a fortresslike prison. Stories about pelicans abounded in the Middle Ages, identifying them with Christ's suffering and leading to their use on medieval heraldry as symbols of charity and piety.

Black-capped Chickadee   *Parus atricapillus*

Although the black-capped chickadee inhabits our northern wood-
lands, it is typical of New England. In Maine, a committee interested
in conservation pushed for its adoption in 1927; Massachusetts chose
it in 1941. This acrobatic bird's tenacity has enabled it to survive the
harsh New England winters despite a high mortality rate. Weighing just
one-half ounce, it puffs out its feathers for insulation and is adept at
nibbling seeds from pinecones or picking dormant insects from frozen
tree limbs. One doesn't have to be a bird-watcher to recognize its call,
chick-a-dee-dee. The birds often nest in birdhouses or tree cavities, and
can be tamed to eat out of one's hand.

Baltimore Oriole   *Icterus galbula*

Maryland's lawmakers chose the Baltimore oriole because, like their flower emblem, the black-eyed Susan, it wears the colors of Lord Baltimore—orange and black. This bird of great beauty originated in the tropics. It is one of the many species of icterids familiar in North America. In the spring, the oriole comes north to build its nest, an impressive pouch six or seven inches deep, woven of grasses, dried roots, and whatever fibers can be obtained. It is said that country women had to guard any threads they were bleaching outside for their weaving. The oriole's pouch is usually hung from the outer branches of a tall tree such as an elm.

Designated in 1947, the oriole (also called the northern oriole) has been celebrated by poets and, as sports fans know, has given its name to Maryland's major league baseball team.

Common Loon *Gavia immer*

In 1961, Minnesota adopted the common loon, a bird legendary for its compelling call and uninhibited crazy laughter. During the breeding season, the male's yodels and wails are sometimes mistaken for wolf howls. One of four living species of primitive northern water birds, the common loon has a torpedo-shaped body well designed for diving and swimming, but it is almost helpless on land. Nests are built a few feet from the wild shores of freshwater lakes and ponds, and parents carry their chicks to and fro on their backs.

Loons are protected under federal law, as are most birds in the United States. Once, large numbers perished from waste oil spilled by ships in coastal waters. Acid rain has also diminished their population. Now conservationists are trying to band and study the birds. But banding them is difficult, as there is a chance of disrupting the nest, and the older birds are wary and elusive.

Eastern Bluebird   *Sialia sialis*

The eastern bluebird has been serving as Missouri's emblem since 1927, but New York waited until 1970 to designate it. In fact, the Empire State, which was the first state in the country to adopt a floral emblem, was the last to choose a bird. Both states chose the most common of the three bluebird species and the only one found east of the Great Plains.

New York's selection is especially meaningful because, until recently, the bluebird had suffered a decline in the state. This was partly due to the bird's peaceful nature and small size, which put it at a disadvantage when competing with more aggressive birds, such as starlings, for nesting sites. To remedy this, Audubon societies and bird clubs encouraged the setting up of special birdhouses, with openings no more than an inch and a half in diameter, along roadways and in areas within the bird's nesting range. Happily, just having a safe place to nest has helped the beautiful bluebird make a strong comeback.

Purple Finch   *Carpodacus purpureus*

New Hampshire's purple finch, designated in 1957, may have been a reminder to its supporters of the state's floral emblem, the purple lilac, chosen many years earlier. Actually, the lovely little male is the one who carries the deep wine coloring; his mate and hatchlings more resemble sparrows. Only dedicated bird-watchers can tell the female purple finch and sparrow apart—the heavier beak, eye stripe, and deeper tail notch of the finch being the distinguishing marks. Finches, especially males, are among the most varied and colorful of birds—all have typical conical beaks adapted to seed eating, and all often warble their songs during their characteristic undulating flight.

Roadrunner   *Geococcyx californianus*

To most people unfamiliar with the Southwest, the roadrunner is known mainly as a cartoon character. And indeed, this large, crested ground bird of the cuckoo family is a curious species. Early pioneers along the Santa Fe Trail first noticed it as it ran ahead in the wheel ruts of the prairie schooners. Today, it can be seen racing automobiles on highways—running on long, stout legs, white-tipped tail streaming behind. A weak flier, the roadrunner lives all year round in the desert and feeds largely on small snakes and lizards, killing its prey by pounding with its heavy beak, and devouring the animal head first.

Despite the cuckoo's notorious reputation of laying its eggs in the nests of other birds, this is true mostly of some old-world species. The roadrunner builds its own nest, often in the branches of the cholla cactus, and cares for its young. New Mexico adopted the roadrunner, sometimes called the chapparal bird, as state emblem in 1949.

Scissortailed Flycatcher   *Tyrannus forficatus*

Oklahoma's scissortailed flycatcher is a native of the south central plains and an appropriate choice for this state, which is the center of its nesting range. A drive pushed by the Tulsa Audubon Society, garden clubs, and bird lovers led to a 1951 resolution citing the bird's "striking and beautiful appearance" and "graceful and attractive" flight. When at rest, the bird can be seen sitting quietly on telephone wires and trees along the roadsides, its long tail feathers hanging straight down. Once in flight, it is transformed into an acrobat, opening and closing its tail in scissorlike movements and making sudden, pivotal turns.

Belonging to a group of birds known as tyrants, the scissortail, in the words of the Oklahoma lawmakers, "commands both respect and admiration."

Ruffed Grouse   *Bonasa umbellus*

Designated in 1931 during the Depression, the ruffed grouse had grass-roots support for economic as well as ornamental reasons. A popular game bird, it summers in woodland clearings and spends the winter in evergreen forests. Although related to turkeys, quails, partridges, and pheasants, it is not a true partridge, though hunters often call it one.

The male grouse's elaborate display to attract his mate commands attention throughout grouse country. He makes a muffled drumming sound, increasing in tempo until it is, as the naturalist John James Audubon observed, "a tremor in the air not unlike distant thunder." For many years, the origin of this courtship sound puzzled observers, but slow-motion pictures confirmed that it results from the bird cupping his wings and rapidly beating the air. The rufflike patches of neck feathers that gave this handsome bird its name bestow a certain dignity on it as well.

Rhode Island Red   *Gallus gallus*

The year 1954, when the Rhode Island red was designated state bird, also marked the hundredth anniversary of the breed in this country. A farmer, Isaac C. Wilbour, known for his chicken farm in Little Compton, sought to improve a breed being developed nearby and, by 1896, advertised his Rhode Island reds—the name he had bestowed on his hardy fowl—in poultry journals. Soon his stock was being shipped and crated across the country and to many other countries as well. At the turn of the century, a monument was erected near the birthplace of this famous breed.

Fowl were probably first domesticated by Bronze Age peoples around 4000 B.C., from a wild jungle species. Today, chickens are raised mostly to produce meat and eggs, while some ornamental varieties are cultivated for exhibition only.

Carolina Wren   *Thryothorus ludovicianus*

For a number of years, South Carolinians recognized the Carolina wren as their state bird. But in 1939, an act was passed designating the mockingbird. This act was repealed in 1948, and the Carolina wren was reinstated as the official bird.

This small, busy bird is present in all areas of the state, from the coast to the lower hillsides, and in fact is common throughout the other eastern states in summer and winter. Garden shrubbery and tree holes are favorite nesting sites. Indeed, any cavity—even the pocket of a shirt hung on a clothesline—affords refuge. The Carolina wren is the largest of the eastern wrens and, like all wrens, feeds mainly on insects and can be recognized by its loud song and dry, scolding rattle.

Ring-necked Pheasant   *Phasianus colchicus*

Pheasants are among the most spectacular birds of the avian kingdom. The species chosen by South Dakota in 1943 was introduced from Asia. It was named *Phasianus colchicus,* the Pheasant of Colchis, because a similar species may have been the one brought back from ancient Colchis to Greece by Jason and the Argonauts on their return from their quest for the Golden Fleece. In this hemisphere, the ring-necked pheasant has acclimatized itself in the plains states of the northern United States and in Canada, where it is at home in open country and on farmlands.

California Gull *Larus californicus*

Deeply rooted in the lore of Utah is the California gull, adopted in 1955. A near famine in Salt Lake City in the last century almost destroyed a Mormon settlement there. The famine was caused by an invasion of locusts that devastated the crops. Then in 1848, California gulls from the Great Salt Lake miraculously appeared and devoured enough insects so the Mormons were finally able to harvest a crop and survive the winter. A grateful citizenry erected a statue to the gulls in Salt Lake City to commemorate this event. The twenty-two-inch gull credited with saving the Mormons' crops—and lives—is a species that breeds on inland lakes and migrates to coastal salt waters for the winter.

It is interesting that Utah's state flower, the elegant sego lily, is also a symbol of life and hope, the bulbs of this plant having saved the Mormons from starvation during the period of famine.

Hermit Thrush *Catharus guttatus*

Thrushes are famous as songbirds, and Vermont's hermit thrush is no exception. Its melodic, flutelike call accompanies farmers during afternoon chore time, which has earned it the nickname of the chore bird. A solitary creature, the hermit thrush usually builds its nest on the forest ground, and its song, lovely as it is, is seldom given except from this safe haven or from a tree branch. The hermit thrush belongs to a group of spotted-breasted thrushes—the wood, Swainson's, and gray-cheeked thrushes and the veery—that inhabit North America. It is our only thrush with the distinctive characteristic of sharply raising and then slowly lowering its tail several times a minute, and is the species most commonly seen in the winter.

Legislation for the adoption of the hermit thrush as state bird was enacted in 1941, despite strong support for other contenders, notably the blue jay and the robin. The Vermont Federation of Women's Clubs had informally made the choice years earlier.

Index of State Birds